The only way to excellence is to consistently improve yourself every single day.
—Thomas J. Vilord

Our business in life is not to get ahead of others, but to of ourselves—to b to outstrip by our
—Stewart B. Johnson

You are unique, and if that is not fulfilled, then something has been lost.
—Martha Graham

Don't limit yourself. Many people limit themselves to what they think they can do. You can go as far as your mind lets you. What you believe, you can achieve!
—Mary Kay Ash

Satisfaction lies in the effort, not in the attainment. Full effort is full victory.
—Mahatma Gandhi

The more a child becomes aware of a parent's willingness to listen, the more a parent will begin to hear.
—Gordon Macdonald

The universe is full of magical things waiting for our wits to grow sharper.
—Eden Phillpotts

Presented By
The
Glenwood Springs
Sunrise Rotary
Club

YOUR SONG

The First Growing Field Adventure

A story of personal strength...

A story about finding your own voice...

A story for all kids about learning to soar!

For information regarding permission, write to Growing Field Books at:
311 Belview Court, Longmont, Colorado 80501
or through *info@growingfield.com*

Publisher's Cataloging-in-Publication
(Provided by Quality Books, Inc.)

Hoog, Mark E.
    Your song: another "growing field" adventure / by
Mark E. Hoog. -- Rev. Ed.
    p. cm.
    SUMMARY: In the magical Growing Field, a young
boy, Maxx, learns he has much in common with Skyler,
a young eagle just learning to fly. Together with a fox,
a lion and a cheetah, Maxx and Skyler discover their
own unique abilities.

    LCCN 2006937446
    ISBN-13: 978-0-9770391-2-8
    ISBN-10: 0-9770391-2-9

1. Self-actualization (Psychology)--Juvenile fiction.
2. Self-esteem--Juvenile fiction. 3. Ability--Juvenile
fiction. [1. Self-esteem--Fiction. 2. Ability--Fiction.]
I. Title.

PZ7.H6335You 2007   [Fic]
                    QBI06-600550
          Printed in China

The Growing Field series was inspired by, and written in memory of,
my colleague, mentor and friend
Jason Dahl—
the Captain of United Flight 93 that crashed in Pennsylvania
on September 11, 2001.
May your voice—and your leadership message—live on forever!

The Growing Field series is dedicated to my twin sister, Michele.
You believed in me—and this series—from the beginning. Thank you.
The world needs more teachers like you! I love you.

Your Song is dedicated to all of those who have ever taken the time
to wrap their arms around a child
to help them soar with the power of their own wings.
—Mark Hoog

To my mom, Trenna,
I am inspired by your love, work with children,
and ability to fly against the strongest winds.
—Rob Aukerman

Each man has his own vocation. The talent is the call. He is like a ship in a river; he runs against obstructions on every side but one, on that side all obstruction is taken away and he sweeps serenely over a deepening channel into an infinite sea. Every man has this call of the power to do something unique and no man has any other call.

–Ralph Waldo Emerson
Self Reliance

The kids in Walden are all very special.

Some have blue eyes, some have brown,
some have light hair and others dark... 5

Some wear glasses and others do not.
Some are fast, some are slow, some are big,
and some are small.

No two kids in Walden are exactly alike.
The children in Walden are unique and spectacular.
The children in Walden are just like you!

The town of Walden is also very special.
It has a magical place called the Growing Field
and a wonderful teacher named Nightingale.
This wise sage has been bringing lessons from
the Growing Field to the children of Walden
for a long time. Join us now,
for our next adventure...

Maxx is the smallest boy
in Walden and he has
a very big question.

"What am I good at? I'm so small, how am I supposed to do anything big?" he asks.

"What are you good at?"
asks Maxx's father, walking up behind him.

"That is a great question!

It reminds me of a story from the Growing Field

I heard when I was your age.

May I share it with you?"

Maxx slid over and made room for his father.
His father sat down and began to speak softly.

"This story is about a young eagle
who wanted to fly more than anything.
This eagle's name was Skyler
and he lived deep in the Growing Field."

"Are you ready for your first
flying lesson, Skyler?"
asked Father Nightingale.

Skyler, peering nervously
out over the canyon,
replied: "I am afraid Father,
and do not think
I am ready to fly."

Father Nightingale hugged his son gently
and said, "Son, somewhere your own gifts
and talents are waiting to be found.
These gifts are yours alone and
make up all that is unique about you.
These talents are Your Song.
When you find Your Song,
you will no longer be afraid
and will be ready to fly."

Skyler told his father,
"I am off to find My Song.
I will look everywhere until I find it!"

While out walking, he met a young fox.

Skyler asked, "Mr. Fox, what is YOUR song?"

19

The fox thought a moment and then said,
"Well, I am very cunning and clever; THAT is MY Song."
"Is that MY song too?" asked Skyler.
"No," said the fox. "You are not
as clever as I am so
that is not Your Song."

"So," Skyler said, "you are not clever
like the fox, or fast like the cheetah,
but you are very strong...
Is that MY song too?" asked Skyler.

"No," said the lion.
"You are not as strong as I am,
so that is not Your Song."

Skyler hung his head
and continued searching for his song.

He walked a long time,
all through the Growing Field,
until it started to get dark.

That night, Skyler said to his father:

"I just don't understand. I looked everywhere
and could not find My Song.
I am still afraid and still cannot fly."

Nightingale smiled warmly at his son and asked,

"Skyler, what scares you?"

"Everywhere I went," explained Skyler, "I met others who were better than me...I am not as clever as Mr. Fox, as fast as Ms. Cheetah or as strong as Mr. Lion.

I walked all day and did not find My Song."

"The problem," explained Nightingale,
"is that you were looking for Your Song in the wrong places.
You can only find Your Song when you look inside yourself."

The young Eagle thought a moment and asked, "You mean the fox,
the cheetah and the lion were wrong about my song?"

Nightingale looked at his son and said,
"They are only right if you believe that they are.
If you believe that you don't
have a special talent,
or can't do something, then you can't.

But if you believe in your heart
that anything is possible,
then THAT will become true."

For the first time, Skyler thought about his own strength and wide, beautiful wings. He turned to his father and said, "I may not be as clever as the fox, but I can see much farther from the air. I may not run as fast as the cheetah, but I can fly faster than she can run. And I may not be as strong as the lion, but he will never be able to fly and touch a cloud."

Nightingale smiled at his son's courage and wisdom. "Everyone in life has their own song," he explained. "Everyone has at least one thing he or she can do better than anyone else...something they are meant to do. It is up to each of us to find our own song and begin singing."

Skyler looked up at his Father and asked, "Father, what is your song?"

"My song is simple," said Nightingale. "My song is to help you find yours!"

The young eagle, now confident
in his own talents and abilities,

SWOOOOSSSHH...

looked down and no longer saw the rocks or dangers below. They were simply obstacles to overcome and fly above. Without hesitation, Skyler walked to the cliff's edge and...

began to soar!

Maxx opened his eyes and smiled at his father. Staring out over the canyon, he realized that he had many unique gifts and talents to share with the world...
he knew where to find his own song.

As Maxx ran back to tell the other kids of Walden about the story of Skyler, he heard his father say:

"I am proud of the young man you are becoming. Like Father Nightingale, it is my job to help you find Your Song. You have so many talents and I am looking forward to watching you soar through life!"

"I love you little eagle."

Discussion Seeds for "Your Song"

It has been said that a musician must make music, an artist must paint and a poet must write if they are to be ultimately at peace with themselves. What humans can be...they must be!

We can introduce our children to the first step in personal growth and development by helping them:

- Recognize that they have a unique gift and talent to share with the world.
- Pursue their unique passions and interests.
- Understand their talents and passions may be different from others'.
- Know that their gift is capable of changing the world.
- Learn to love the life long process of self-discovery and personal growth.

Every child is born with a spectacular gift. Every day is an opportunity to soar as you and your child discover **Your Song.**

Acknowledgments

Special thanks to:

—Rob Aukerman for believing in this project and bringing it to life.

—The magical Lisa Conner at Matchbox Studio for graphic design brilliance.

—The dazzling William Roth for layout editing.

—Ann Diaz for unending editing patience.

—My parents, brother, teachers and friends who helped nurture the Growing Field seed;
There are too many of you to list, but a little of each of you
can be found in every Growing Field adventure.

—Most importantly my wonderful wife Kristi and three spectacular kids:
Branson, Morgan and Mitchell. You have each loved me when I needed it most...every day!

A portion of all proceeds are donated to the Jason Dahl Scholarship fund.

A portion of all Growing Field proceeds are donated to the Children's Leadership Institute
for the promotion of youth leadership and character education.

Read what others are saying about their magical journey through the Growing Field...

Growing Field
Where children go to grow

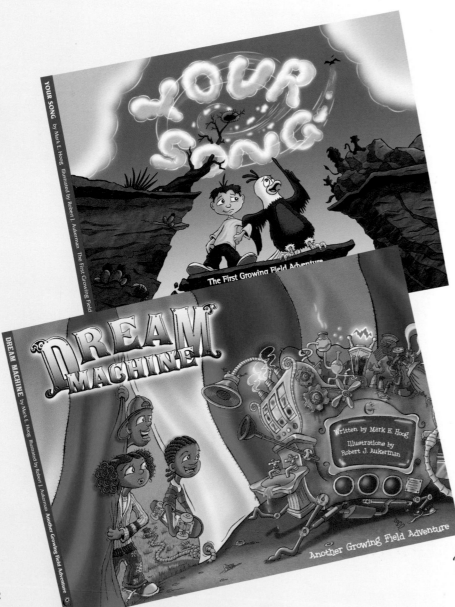

Richard Riley   U.S. Secretary of Education   1993-2001

"A walk through the Growing Field is a wonderful and creative way for any adult to help grow a child's self-esteem, character and love of reading. Everyone can benefit from the seeds to be found in the Growing Field."

W. Mitchell   Top Motivational Speaker U.S./Australia

"Mark Hoog is doing the most important work in America today—growing our children. With *Magic and Treasure* and *Dreams and Songs and Gifts* he's helping them learn to lead. Mark's work is one of the best gifts you can give both children and adults. *The Growing Field* series MUST be the next thing you read and share with others."

Brian Tracy   Top author/business success coach

"The Growing Field books show you how to encourage, inspire and motivate your children to become happy, successful adults."

Plant the seeds today...

Learn more: www.GrowingField.com

If you enjoyed this book, you'll also enjoy Dream Machine, the second book in the Growing Field Leadership Book series.

Dream Machine ...a story for dreamers of all ages.

Invited into the magical Walden carnival by a familiar gypsy, Jazzmin and her two brothers come face to face with Nightingale's magical Dream Machine. Working to bring this crazy contraption to life, each child finds the key to their wildest dreams was in their hands all along.

Now my friends, your Dream Machine awaits.

What are your dreams and what will make them terrific?

Let your journey continue...

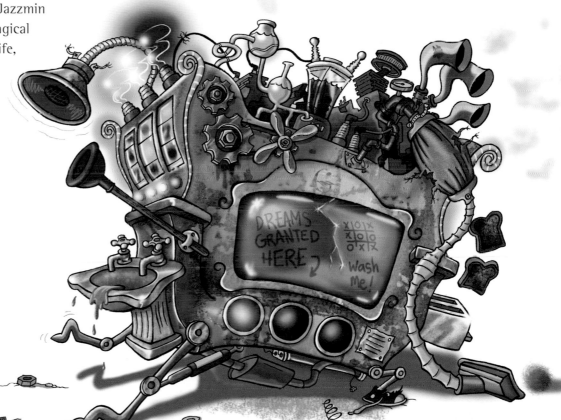

Leadership Seeds:

- Dream creation
- Goal visualization
- Life achievement

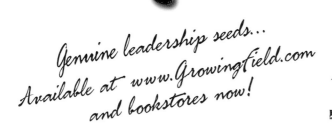

Genuine leadership seeds... Available at www.GrowingField.com and bookstores now!

Start building your very own collection of Growing Field inspirational, motivational books today!
Online orders: www.GrowingField.com

Let him who would move the world, first move himself.
—Socrates

When these parenting years have passed, something precious will have flickered and gone out of my life. Thus, I am resolved to enjoy every day that remains in the parenting era.

Argue for your limitations and sure enough, they're yours.
—Richard Bach

It's time for us all to stand and cheer for the doer, the achiever— the one who recognizes the challenges and does something about it.
—Vince Lombardi

The benefit of your toils are not what you get, but rather what they make you become.

Some people dream of success... while others wake up and work hard at it.

What you think about yourself is much more important than what others think of you.
—Marcus Annaeus Seneca

In the pursuit of a dream, the best path will often span the deepest ravine. One can never consent to creep when one feels an impulse to soar.
—Helen Keller

The best way to predict the future... is to create it.

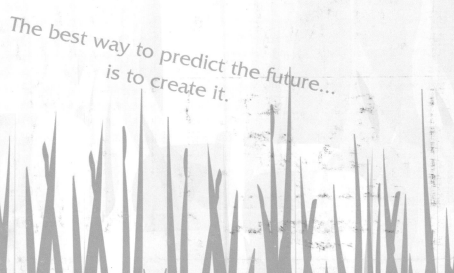